First published by Parragon in 2010

Parragon
Queen Street House
4 Queen Street
Bath, BA1 1HE, UK

ISBN 978-1-4075-8433-1
Printed in China

Winnie the Pooh

SOMEBODY'S TREASURE

By K. Emily Hutta

Illustrated by
Carson Van Osten, John Kurtz
& the Disney Storybook Artists

Bath New York Singapore Hong Kong Cologne Delhi Melbourne

It was springtime in the Hundred-Acre Wood. The flowers were budding, the birds were chirping, and Winnie the Pooh was doing a bit – really just a very little bit – of spring-cleaning.

"One. . . thing. . . at a time," Pooh said to himself, puffing as he bent over his somewhat-rounder-than-average tummy to pick up a cracked honeypot. "I'll just put this pot outside for now. That will be quite enough spring-cleaning for one day."

As Pooh stepped out his front door, balancing the pot and trying very hard not to tip over, a cheery voice called out to him.

"Hello, Pooh," Kanga said, waving.

"Halloooo," Pooh said. He tried to wave back, but the pot teetered wildly and he had to use both hands to keep it from falling.

"I'm getting rid of this useless old thing," Pooh explained. "A honeypot that won't hold honey is no good to me."

"Oh, may I have it?" Kanga asked. "I can use it as a planter for my spring flowers!"

"Yes!" Pooh said eagerly. "But it's cracked, you know." Pooh believed a bear should always be honest about such things.

"Oh, that's good," Kanga said.

"It is?" Pooh asked, quite surprised.

"The cracks will let extra water run out," Kanga said. "That's just what a planter should do."

Pooh waved until Kanga was out of sight. "Who could have guessed that my useless old pot would turn out to be Kanga's perfect new planter?" Pooh asked himself. When no one answered, he shrugged. Some things were just meant to remain mysteries.

Suddenly, a loud grumble sounded from somewhere close by. Pooh nodded. "I see what you mean," he said to his tummy. "Spring-cleaning does make a bear awfully hungry. I think it may be – in fact I'm quite certain it is – time for a little smackerel."

While Pooh was busy licking honey from his paws, Kanga was walking past Rabbit's house.

Rabbit was sitting in the sun, brushing his tail and muttering.

"Did you say something, Rabbit?" Kanga asked.

"I said that this happens every spring," Rabbit complained. "When I clear the weeds from my garden patch, I get thistles in my tail and holes in my coveralls."

"Well, when you're finished brushing your tail, why don't you come to my house," Kanga said kindly. "I can sew patches on those coveralls for you."

Rabbit brushed and brushed until every thistle was pulled out, along with quite a bit of soft, puffy fur from his tail.

"Rather nice, if I do say so myself," Rabbit said, admiring his reflection in the window. "Now if Kanga can help me patch my coveralls, I'll be as good as new."

As soon as Rabbit left, a shy little bird swooped down and gathered some of the soft fluff from Rabbit's brush. She flew with it to a nearby tree where she was building a nest.

Back and forth she went until she had the coziest nest in the Hundred-Acre Wood. Her chicks would be so snug and warm – and all because Rabbit had got thistles in his tail!

Kanga was busy sorting through her sewing basket when Rabbit arrived at her house. She pointed to a small pile of brightly coloured fabric scraps.

"These bits and pieces are left over from some of the sewing projects I did over the winter," Kanga said. "Don't you think they'll be just right for your patches?"

"Oh, yes!" Rabbit cried. "And these would make great pockets for my apron!" he said, sorting through the bright squares of fabric. "And this one would be perfect for a new hankerchief! Oh, how am I going to decide?"

"Take them all," Kanga said, laughing. "I don't need them. I'm happy to find someone who can use them."

With fresh patches sewn onto his coveralls and his pockets stuffed with, well, with more patches, Rabbit was headed toward home when he bumped into Eeyore.

"I'm terribly sorry," Eeyore said. "I don't know how I overlooked you with all of those, those, ummmm . . ."

"They're patches. And pockets. And this one is a hankerchief," Rabbit said proudly. "Kanga gave them to me."

Eeyore studied his friend for a long moment. "They're surprisingly cheerful," Eeyore said. "I don't suppose Kanga has anything I could use to brighten things up for spring."

"Brighten things up? You?" Rabbit said doubtfully. "Well, I guess it can't hurt to try."

And so it was that Eeyore visited Kanga that morning, too. And if it took him a rather longish time to choose from among Kanga's leftover ribbons – even with all the helpful advice he got from Roo – well, no one was in any sort of hurry anyway.

It was early afternoon in the Hundred-Acre Wood by the time Eeyore walked by Piglet's house. Piglet was sweeping a pile of haycorn caps out the door.

"Something's different about you, Eeyore," said Piglet.

"I've gotten a little spruced up for spring," Eeyore said.

"You look splendid!" Piglet said. "You look like you could be going to a party! In fact, a party is a very good idea. That is, I've made enough haycorn muffins for a party – if only I had a picnic table where everyone could sit. It would be a shame to sit inside on such a lovely spring day. Don't you agree, Eeyore?"

"Yes," Eeyore said, nodding slowly. "And I think maybe I can help."

A short while later, Piglet was amazed to see a large wooden crate coming down the path toward his house. The crate had an assortment of legs, one rather sproingy-looking tail and writing on the side that said "FRADGIL." Piglet ran inside and peeked through a crack in his door, just in case the crate was up to no good.

"Hoo-hoo-hoo!" the crate shouted as it got closer. "Where are you?"

Piglet was too frightened to answer.

"I just knew this would happen," the crate said in a completely different and somewhat gloomy voice. "He was here a little while ago and now he's gone."

"Yes, well, perhaps if we put this down, we'll be able to find him," the crate said rather sensibly.

Piglet watched wide-eyed as the crate tilted to the side, and out came Tigger, Eeyore and Owl!

"Oh, it's you!" Piglet cried happily, running outside to greet them.

"Well, who did you think it was?" Tigger asked.

Piglet really couldn't say.

"Owl got an enormmormerous box of books the other day, and he doesn't need the crate anymore," Tigger said. "Don't you think it will make a splend-iferous picnic table?"

"Oh, yes!" Piglet said. "If you would put it down right over there, I'll invite the rest of our friends for haycorn muffins and tea."

In no time at all, Piglet's friends were gathered around his splendid new picnic table enjoying a springtime mid-afternoon tea party.

"You must have been baking all morning," Pooh said politely. But what actually came out was, "Moo muf huf bibakeen ow mowmin." Because, as everyone knows, it is difficult for a bear to pronounce his words properly with a mouth full of haycorn muffin.

Owl noticed the pile of haycorn caps outside Piglet's door. "Those would be just the thing to make new checkers for my checkers set," Owl said. "Let's try them out, Roo. Most of mine rolled through the cracks and bounced out the windows when I played checkers with Tigger over the winter."

"Well, a tigger has to bounce once in a while," Tigger said. "Even if he is playing checkers."

The friends lingered long into the soft light of evening. It had been such a wonderful day – such a surprising and useful sort of day – that no one wanted it to end.

Piglet sighed happily, admiring the way his friends fit around his new table. Rabbit and Eeyore looked so festive in their new finery. Kanga was chatting about her new planter. Owl was playing checkers on the tablecloth with Roo. And absolutely everyone seemed to be enjoying Piglet's delicious haycorn muffins – especially Winnie the Pooh.